CHILDREN'S CHOICES

By Lola M. Jones

I would like to thank my grandchildren,
Lee Diamond Stewart and Anthony Stewart Jr. for their interest, their suggestions,
and their wise choices in the production of this book.
Special thanks to my image consultant, Beverly Willis, whose choices made our stories come alive.

A FUN DAY FOR ROBBIE RABBIT

"There's nothing to do," Robbie Rabbit said to no one in particular. His long white ears drooped. His bushy tale sagged. He poked around the rose bushes. He sniffed at the marigolds. He scrambled over the white picket fence next to his house. Just then he noticed Mrs. Rabbit in her kitchen next door. Maybe I could go play a trick on Mrs. Rabbit, thought Robbie with a mischievous tilt of his head. That would be something to do today.

At that moment Mrs. Rabbit was taking three carrot pies out of the oven. She placed them at the open window to cool. Mrs. Rabbit smiled as she went upstairs to get dressed for the church bazaar. She felt happy with her pies.

Robbie Rabbit came skipping across Mrs. Rabbit's back yard. He was looking for something fun to do today. Suddenly he spied the pies on the window sill. He wiggled his pink nose. "Aah the wonderful smell of carrot pies he thought. He stood perfectly still on his two back legs and wiggled his nose once more. His floppy white ears came to attention. Before he knew it , he hopped up on the window sill and snatched one of the pies.

Sparkie the sparrow saw him from her perch in the tree. " Stop, stop that's not your pie" she scolded. But Robbie Rabbit bounded away, laughing at his adventure.

Callie the cow mooed her displeasure. "That's not your pie," she called. Robbie. Rabbit simply scurried between her legs and hurried on his way.

Little lamb looked up as Robbie Rabbit ducked under a bush. "That is not your pie, " she said. Robbie Rabbit paid no attention.

He ran excitedly through the tall grass to a cozy hole in a large oak tree. This was his favorite hiding place. He sat down at last, gasping for breath. It was safe here.

Robbie heard no voices except the small voice in his heart. "This is not my pie" the voice said. Robbie Rabbit felt sad.

" This is no fun" he thought. Then he picked up the pie and marched straight to Mrs. Rabbit's front door." I'm sorry I took your pie," he said sheepishly."

"Well I'm glad you brought it back," replied Mrs. Rabbit in surprise. Would you like to come to the bazaar with me? There'll be games and prizes and plenty of pie."

Robbie Rabbit's grey eyes lit up expectantly. His long white ears perked up. His pink nose wiggled more than ever. "Yes, Ma'am, I would" he replied joyfully.

At last he found something fun to do today.

SABRINA'S SURPRISE

"Momma, what can I take for the potluck?" Sabrina called as she rushed into the kitchen and dropped her books on the table. It was ethnic week at Mack school and all the fifth graders were to bring a dish for the family potluck Friday night. " Momma what can I take?" Sabrina repeated in an even higher pitched tone.

"We'll see, Sabrina " Momma said absently as she continued folding the laundry. "Come and help me sort these socks." Sabrina hated it when Momma said "we'll see." That usually meant that Momma did not want to deal with it right then. The potluck was just two days away.

"Can I go now Momma " Sabrina asked as she placed the last two socks in the basket, thankful that they came out even. "Yes, and take Mandy with you, You know she needs to go out."

"But Momma, it's Terrell's turn . . .Sabrina's voice faded behind Momma's warning glance.

Sabrina got the leash from the door knob and called Mandy. The air was fresh and cool as Sabrina walked down Summit Street with Mandy at her heels. Sabrina's mind drifted once again to the potluck. Today at school the kids were talking about what they were making for the potluck.

Joe bragged that his father was helping him to make lasagna from an old family recipe. Sabrina wished she could bring something from Daddy's home, something Jamaican.

As Sabrina turned down Fountain Street, Mandy suddenly gave a yank to the leash and in two seconds she was running down the street chasing a black and white cat. Now Sabrina would have to catch Mandy!

The last time the dog ran away a neighbor had complained that Mandy had turned over her garbage can. Momma warned her not to let this happen again. Sabrina raced after the dog yelling for her to come back. Mandy kept on going till her leash got caught in Mrs. Johnson's back fence. Sabrina, quite out of breath, rang the bell.

" You' dog run away again, eh" Mrs. Johnson said smiling. "Yes, M' am. Can I go around the back and get her?" "Sure you can, ma love. Bring her round here an let me give her some water." "Sit down an calm yourself, child " Mrs. Johnson coaxed after the rescue.

Mandy lapped up the water seeming quite pleased with her adventure. Sabrina listened to Mrs. Johnson's lilting accent. It reminded her of Daddy. She began to feel better. She remembered hearing that Mrs. Johnson was from Jamaica. Sabrina knew that was where Daddy came from.

"Mrs. Johnson, would you tell me about Jamaica?" Sabrina asked. Mrs. Johnson's face seemed to light up. She enjoyed having this visitor who reminded her of her own grand daughter back home in Jamaica. The next day Sabrina walked Mandy straight over to Mrs. Johnson's house. She spent all afternoon there.

That afternoon Sabrina asked her mother if she could invite Mrs. Johnson to the potluck. "Sure ,Baby, Momma said, " but what are you going to take? We better get started fixing something"

"That's ok , Momma" It's all set" replied Sabrina, her eyes dancing with secret pleasure.

That evening Sabrina, Momma, Terrell, and Mrs. Johnson walked into the gym at Mack school where a long table was spread with foods from many lands.

Sabrina proudly uncovered a large casserole of Jamaican curried oxtails and rice which she had prepared with Mrs. Johnson's help. Momma said she was proud of her.

Sabrina hugged Mrs. Johnson, "You can be my Grandma from now on" she said.

BOBBY'S DREAM

Bobby tossed the ball through the net one more time. He had been shooting baskets by himself ever since he came home from school. He ran to greet his father as the car pulled into the driveway.

"Dad, can you come to school tomorrow?" Bobby asked, following his father into the house.

"I don't know, Bobby. Let me take off my coat and we'll talk about it." Mr. Jordan hung his coat and hat in the hall closet and gave Bobby a surprise toss. This brought a reluctant smile to Bobby's serious face as he caught the ball.

Bobby was small for his age. His thin brown face seemed lost behind his horn-rimmed glasses. His two front teeth protruded slightly when he smiled. Bobby has not felt like smiling lately. He was new at Perry School. His dream is to play on the fourth grade basketball team after school, but the kids think he is too small. Bobby is sure he can do it if they would just give him a chance.

Mrs. Jordan calls out, "Is that you, Bob? Dinner is ready." Bobby and Mr. Jordan wash their hands and go to the table. "Dad, can you come?" Bobby asked again as soon as Mr. Jordan finished saying the blessing. "What's this all about, son?" Mr. Jordan asked. "I'd like you to tell my class about how you knew Martin Luther King. They don't believe me."

Bobby's eyes cloud over. He remembers the teasing of his classmates when he told them that his father had known Martin Luther King. Are you kidding?" David had said in disbelief. "He did not," Roger had said emphatically. "Martin Luther King is in history. Your father couldn't know him.

"Why do you want me to come to school, Bobby?" Mr. Jordan repeated.

"We are doing reports about famous Americans. Mine is on Martin Luther King. The teacher says we can bring in visual aids," Bobby says, carefully pronouncing the new words. Mr. Jordan bursts into laughter. "Am I to be a visual aid?" he asks, amused. "I don't think I have ever been a visual aid before." "But . . . perhaps I can help your friends to see what Martin Luther King stands for," said Mr. Jordan, becoming more serious. "I'll call your teacher."

The next day Mr. Jordan took his lunch break at one o'clock instead of twelve. He arrived at Bobby's school just as the afternoon class began. Bobby proudly introduced his father. Bobby and his classmates eagerly listened to stories about Martin Luther King as a boy. They learned that Dr. King had been the youngest and the smallest in his class. Because of his skill and determination, he made the basketball team.

At dinner that evening Mrs. Jordan asked, "How was school today?"

"Great' said Bobby. "I've been practicing with David and Roger. Maybe I'll make the team after all." Mr. and Mrs. Jordan exchange smiles.

ABBEY

Abbey took 5 plates from the cupboard and began to set the table for dinner. "Abbey, put an extra cup of beans in the pot", Momma said. "We having company, Momma?" Abbey asked. ""No questions, Abbey". Hurry up with the beans and cut up some more potatoes for the soup pot" Abbey liked having company. Why was Momma so cross, she wondered.? Having company was rare since they moved out to the edge of town last year. Perhaps the pastor from Bethel would be coming with his daughter Sadie. She and Sadie could . . . Abbey's thoughts were interrupted by Momma's voice.

"Do what I told you, Abbey. No time for foolishness tonight."

"You want me to set an extra place?" Abbey continued hopefully. Momma looked troubled and Abbey wanted to ask her why, but she suddenly hugged her mother instead. Momma returned her hug, then pushed her away gently. "Come on now, Abbey. Help Daniel and Faith get washed for supper"

Somehow Abbey new that what Momma needed was more than helping her younger brother and sister, but Abbey didn't know what it was. She filled the basin and began scrubbing their hands and face.

There was no sign of company when Pa came home from his job at the foundry. Pa said a long blessing, more like he would say on Sundays. He asked the Lord to protect them and any strangers that should come to their door. He prayed for strength and wisdom in these trying times. Daniel and Faith had stories to tell about the new teacher on Hill Street. Pa was strangely quiet all through supper.

"We'll not be going to mid-week service tonight" he announced after the meal. "Abbey, take the children upstairs and hear their prayers before bed. And mind you do your own praying too."

Abbey's heart sank. She was supposed to sing a solo at church this evening. She had been practicing for two weeks. She wondered if Pa had forgotten. She gave him a sideways glance under her lowered eyelids. Something in his expression stopped the question on her lips. "Yes, Pa" was all she said as she swallowed hard to hold back her tears.

Upstairs Abbey heard the children's prayers absently. Pa had taken the cart out on Ann Arbor Trail right after supper. Now Abbey heard muffled sounds from the barn. She climbed on the chest and looked out the small window of the bedroom she shared with her brother and sister. There was no light in the barn which stood a few yards away.

As she peered into the darkness she saw four shadowy figures slip towards the barn. Abbey became alarmed. She decided to fetch her father. Then she realized that the tall man leading the group was Pa himself.

He was followed by a large woman with a dark shawl over her head and shoulders. Two others, a woman and child followed closely. The child, about Abbey's age looked cold. She had no cloak against the sharp October air.

Abbey climbed down from her perch at the window, puzzled by what she had seen. What could it mean? First there was the extra food, then they did not go to service. Pastor would want her to account for that. And now, strangers in the barn.

Abbey crept to the top of the stairs and listened. The floor creaked as she leaned over the banister, but her parents were too engrossed in their own conversation to hear her.

"Josh, I don't want no parts of it." Her mother said. "We come too far to risk it all now." "Martha, the Lord sent them to us and we've got to help."

Abbey was astonished. She had never before heard her mother speak up in contradiction to her father. This must be serious! She shifted her right foot which had gone to sleep.

"Abbey, come down here" Pa had heard her! As she entered the kitchen, Abbey saw a tall woman with a dark bony face, and deep set eyes, seated at the table.

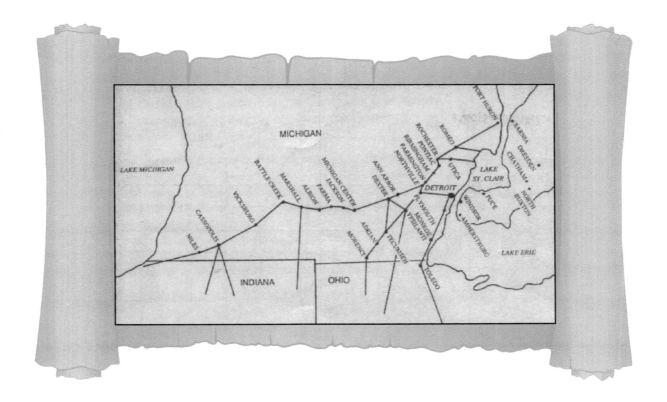

"Mind your manners, Abbey" Momma nudged her. "Howdy, Ma'am, " said Abbey coming to her senses. The woman seated at the table took Abbey's hand in both of hers and smiled at her. She then turned back to Pa and said "We've got to take the Port Huron route, The Windsor route is too dangerous right now" Pa turned to Abbey and said "Sit here with your mother. I'm going to take Mrs. Tubman to the Preacher. Watch close. Don't let anyone in."

Abbey and her mother exchanged fearful glances. Pa was leaving. Momma was fearful. Now Abbey understood. These were fugitive slaves! She knew that she must be strong and follow Pa's instructions. She felt proud that her father trusted her to help. She moved closer to her mother's side.

As Mrs. Tubman rose from the chair to go with Pa, Abbey noticed her slight limp. "Where are the people?' Abbey asked after Pa and Mrs. Tubman left.

"In the closet under the stairs Momma whispered. It's too cold in the barn." Abbey clung to her Mother for a moment. They both were aware of the consequence if they were caught helping fugitive slaves. They also knew that the danger to the little family in the closet would be even greater. They would be whipped and returned to slavery.

Abbey spooned up the soup in two bowls. She buttered two chunks of bread. She moved cautiously towards the closet and handed in the bowls. Two pairs of eyes looked out at her. The woman nodded. Not a word was exchanged. Suddenly there was a banging at the front door and Constable Zebbs was calling for Pa to open the door.

"Pa ain't here" Abbey said opening the door a crack. Momma shook her head in agreement. Abbey had seen the constable many times at the Farmers Market and patrolling in town .But tonight was different. There was a rough looking man with a beard and a moustache at his side.

"You seen any strangers round here this evening?" the constable demanded. "Let's have a look around" Momma looked frightened . . . They were about to come in. Abbey knew she had to do something. "There were some people near the barn earlier" she said. "About an hour ago. I saw them from the window."

Soon Pa and Mrs Tubman returned. Abbey was sent to bed. As she lay next to her sleeping brother and sister she thought about the bravery of the people under the stairs. They had endured all sorts of danger to find freedom.

Abbey got out of bed and opened a small chest. She took out her warm coat that the Quakers had given her. She looked at it for a moment.

Once more Abbey crept down the stairs and thrust the coat into the darkness of the closet. This time a hand pressed hers No words were spoken. Abbey slipped back into bed and silently prayed for the safety of the travelers under the stairs.

Made in the USA
Lexington, KY
02 November 2012